This Little Tiger book belongs to:

_____

_____

_____

With thanks to T.J., T.J., C.J. and P.J. – S. U.

LITTLE TIGER PRESS LTD,
an imprint of the Little Tiger Group
1 The Coda Centre, 189 Munster Road, London SW6 6AW
www.littletiger.co.uk • First published in Great Britain 2011
This edition published 2017
Text and illustrations copyright © Sam Usher 2011
Sam Usher has asserted his right to be identified as the author and illustrator
of this work under the Copyright, Designs and Patents Act, 1988
All rights reserved • ISBN 978-1-84869-718-8
Printed in China • LTP/2700/1848/0417
2 4 6 8 10 9 7 5 3 1

by Sam Usher

Can You See SASSOON?

LITTLE TIGER

This is **Sassoon.** He likes to hide.
Can you find him? Look inside!

Bobbing balloons are floating by,
Soaring slowly through the sky.

Can you see Sassoon there, too,
Hiding away from me and you?

WHAT a picnic!
Ham with custard,
Cheese with icing,
jelly and mustard.

Sassoon is hiding. Can you see?
He's peeking out at you and me.

A pile of presents!
What's inside?
An elephant?
A waterslide?

I can't see him here—can you?
Perhaps Sassoon is
wrapped up, too!

Sailing in the summer sun,
There's a boat for everyone!

WHAT a busy boating lake!
We'll never see that silly snake.

Spotty leggings, fancy frocks,
Frilly dresses, stripy socks.

Giant pants flap in the air.
But where's Sassoon?
He MUST be there!

Spots and stripes
and peeking eyes.
There are toys of
every size.

Oh, dear!
I can't begin to guess
Where he can be
in all this mess!

Where is he now? In outer space!
He's joined a speedy rocket race.

I can see the stars and moon,
But where, oh, where,
are YOU, Sassoon?

So many books,
all full of fun!
I want to stay
and read each one.

Sassoon! Come out!
Where have you gone?
This game has gone on
much too long!

ALL his friends are hiding now!
We have to find him here, but HOW?
Shhhh, everyone! Here's what we'll do:
Let's creep up quietly, ready—

More fantastic stories from Little Tiger Press!

The Littlest Owl

Caroline Pitcher
Tina Macnaughton

Can You See SASSOON?

Sam Usher

Time for Bed, Little One

Caroline Pitcher · Tina Macnaughton

Mighty mo

Alison Brown

The Dark, Dark Night

M. Christina Butler
Jane Chapman

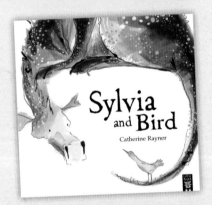

Sylvia and Bird

Catherine Rayner

Rhino's Great BIG Itch!

Natalie Chivers

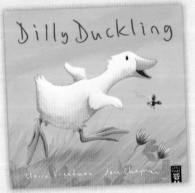

Ready for Bed!

Jane Johnson
Gaby Hansen

Dilly Duckling

Claire Freedman · Jane Chapman

Tracey Corderoy · Alison Edgson

Just One More!

For information regarding any
of the above titles or for our catalog, please contact us:
Little Tiger Press, 1 The Coda Centre, 189 Munster Road, London SW6 6AW, UK
Tel: +44 (0)20 7385 6333 • E-mail: contact@littletiger.co.uk
www.littletiger.co.uk